O'Brien Press Memo
From: The Management
To: All Members of Staff
Subject: The Forbidden Files

You're probably wondering why you arrived this morning to find the police searching your desks.

The safe containing the Forbidden Files was broken into. The Files have been STOLEN.

The stories in these Files were kept locked up and hidden away for good reason. These stories are too FRIGHTENING, too DISTURBING or just too downright DISGUSTING to be read by children.

The police will want to speak to all of you — please give them your full cooperation. We have to find The Forbidden Files; they must NEVER see the light of day.

TOO LATE, SUCKERS!

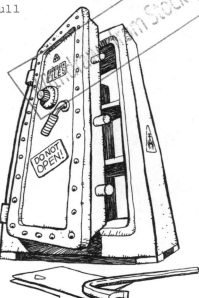

Police file:
Missing person

CONOR KOSTICK, the historian and writer of books for The O'Brien Press, has **disappeared**. He was last seen going in to the ancient manuscripts' library of Trinity College, Dublin, muttering: 'At last, I've found it. It's mine, all **mine**!'

The case is being treated as **very** suspicious.

THE BOOK OF CURSES

Conor Kostick

Illustrated by Julie Parker

THE O'BRIEN PRESS
DUBLIN

First published 2007 by The O'Brien Press Ltd,
12 Terenure Road East, Dublin 6, Ireland.
Tel: +353 1 4923333; Fax: +353 1 4922777
E-mail: books@obrien.ie
Website: www.obrien.ie

ISBN: 978-1-84717-055-2

British Library Cataloguing-in-Publication Data
Kostick, Conor, 1964-
The book of curses. - (Forbidden files)
1. Magic - Juvenile fiction 2. Children's stories
I. Title II. Parker, Julie
823.9'2[J]

1 2 3 4 5 6 7 8 9
07 08 09 10 11

The O'Brien Press
receives assistance from

Layout and design: The O'Brien Press Ltd
Printed in the UK by CPI Bookmarque, Croydon, CR0 4TD

CONTENTS

For Conor and Juno

1

Make A Wish

2

But Is It Cursed?

A very long time ago, Janus, a god with two faces, made two magic books. One let the hopes of its owner come true. This was *The Book of Wishes*. But to make fun of mortals, Janus also made a second book. The second book looked exactly like *The Book of Wishes*. It had the same big red leather covers, the same gold writing and the same thick pages. But it was full of black, wicked magic. It was *The Book of Curses*.

3

The Boy Who **Never** Did What He Was Told

Alex Zwick was the most annoying boy in his school. He was the sort of boy who *never* did what he was told.

At first, his teacher, Miss Jones, had tried to be patient with Alex. But it was no good. You just couldn't make him do anything he didn't want to do. Nor could you stop him getting into trouble: such as the time he ate twenty-four jam tarts for a bet. Or the time he filled his desk with spiders and worms, to see if the spiders would eat the worms (they didn't).

In the end, Miss Jones rang Alex's mum and dad to tell them how hard it was to make him behave. It took a long time to get hold of his parents. They were always away somewhere on the other side of the world. But, eventually, Miss Jones got hold of them in China.

When Alex's parents heard what he'd been up to, they just laughed.

'That boy's first word was "no" and he's never stopped using it since,' explained Alex's mum.

After that Miss Jones almost gave up on Alex Zwick. Sometimes she just looked at him and rolled her eyes up, shaking her head.

*   *   *

One Wednesday, Alex was in trouble again. But, he told himself, it wasn't really his fault. If Moira Walshe hadn't ducked, the elastic band he'd fired wouldn't have hit Miss Jones on the breast.

Shocked, teacher and pupil stared at each other, while the rest of the class held their breath.

When Miss Jones finally spoke, you could see she'd just counted to ten.

'Eight, nine, ten,' her lips whispered.

'Alex Zwick. You must not shoot elastic bands. Do you understand?'

'No,' Alex replied, instinctively. And for that he was banned from a class trip to the museum. Instead, he was on his own in the school library.

Anyway, who wanted to go to the smelly museum? Not Alex Zwick, that's for sure. It wasn't like they had dinosaurs or anything interesting.

So there he was, in the library, bored. *Very* bored.

There were no rules to break. No spiders to catch. If only he had a tennis ball, he could turn one of the shelves into a goal and play football. But, Alex sighed aloud, he didn't have a tennis ball. He had nothing, and there was nothing to do.

Just when Alex was beginning to feel sorry for himself and wonder what his class were all doing, the strip lights in the library roof flickered. For a moment the room went dark. The hair on Alex's head stood up. And down in the darkest corner of the room Alex saw, for the first time, a large and peculiar book.

It's probably a rubbish book, Alex told himself, and football or computer games were miles better than looking at books. But this book, at least, was really big, with thick, deep red leather covers.

It took both hands to lift the strange volume from under the shelf, where it must have been lying for some time, because it was covered in dust.

With a big breath, Alex blew the dust away. Weirdly, the book had no title, just a shiny gold engraving of two faces: one smiling, one crying.

The spine of the book creaked as he opened the heavy leather cover; the thick pages inside all rose up a little, like he was pulling back an accordion, ready to play music.

The book was a total disappointment though. The pages were all empty. Well, except for the very first page, which said in huge golden letters:

What Is It That
You Wish For?

Even though he shouldn't, Alex Zwick often wrote in books. He liked to draw pictures of children hanging with a rope around their necks and his classmates' names next to them. Planes flying along the top of pages, dropped bombs down the margins, with explosions so big that you couldn't read the words at the bottom of the page.

This book was asking to be written on.

First he took out his black pen and drew a spider, with venom dripping from its fangs.

Then he took out his red pen and designed a pit trap, with spikes at the bottom.

While he thought some more, he scribbled a few evil gnome figures in the margins.

Lastly, he took out his green pen and in big letters wrote: I want a brand new games console .

Somewhere, he thought he heard a chuckle: a rather sinister chuckle.

*   *   *

At lunchtime, especially because he wasn't supposed to, Alex Zwick left school and went to the shop to buy crisps. When he finished the crisps, there was no bin nearby, so he dropped the packet on the pavement, even though he knew he shouldn't. Feeling pleased, Alex strolled back along the path towards school.

A moment later a lorry thundered past, going far too fast for the small street. It couldn't stop at the traffic lights and swerved, trying to miss a car coming from its left. With a tremendous crash, the lorry smashed straight into a florist's shop window. Another huge crunch came a second afterwards as the car smacked into the side of the stuck lorry.

Fire and oil ran along the road from the wreckage. The drivers staggered away, waving at those people who were watching with amazement.

'Keep back! Keep back!'

Boom!

A blast of hot air made Alex stagger. He was dizzy from the loud explosion. Bits of metal, plastic and cardboard were swirling all around, some of them burning. People were screaming; alarms were blaring. And a box, thrown out of the truck from the explosion, skidded along the ground, to end up right at his feet.

Playbox. Console and three games included.

'Awesome,' said Alex happily to himself as he picked up the box and walked off.

Behind him was a scene of utter devastation as people stood up slowly and stared at the wreckage.

4

Knock ... Knock ...

Alex Zwick was honest enough to admit that he had a lot of bad traits. But he was no fool. In fact he was downright smart. It was that book. The book was magic. It really worked.

All that afternoon Alex had a very happy time thinking about wishes. What would you wish for? The possibilities were endless and very pleasant to think about. Did he want to be a superstar in a band? A fantastic footballer? Did he want to get top marks in school tests? Or have an endless supply of jam tarts?

As soon as school ended, Alex surprised everyone by asking Miss Jones would she open the library for him.

'Certainly, Alex. Is it a book you want? Don't be long.'

'Oh I won't.'

He hurried over to the darkest corner of the room, out of sight, dragged the huge leather book out and quickly wrote on a blank page:

I want to be rich.

Above him, or was it below? Someone laughed a wicked laugh.

Then he closed the big covers of the magic tome and pushed it right back, far under the shelf, so no one else would see it. To avoid questions from his teacher, who was waiting at the desk, he grabbed a book from the nearest shelf and hurried back.

'*Jill and the Fairy*?' Miss Jones looked at the cover, then regarded Alex with utter suspicion. He just shrugged and raised his eyebrows innocently.

When Alex got home and let himself in, the house was quiet. This was odd. Alex lived with his granny, who fussed over him all the time. She didn't seem to mind that he was the most annoying boy in the world. Normally she would hurry over, take his school bag and ask him what his day had been like.

There was a frantic knocking at the front door. It was their neighbour, Mrs O'Neill.

'What do you want?' Alex asked Mrs O'Neill with a cross voice.

Alex had many reasons for not liking Mrs O'Neill, but the main one was the way she got so upset over her stupid garden gnomes.

One morning, Mrs O'Neill had woken up to see her gnomes lying all over the garden surrounded by streamers, empty beer cans and dolls in party dresses. That was bad enough. But the day she found her smiley fisherman gnome swinging from a tree, with a rope around his neck, was worse. An executioner gnome in a sinister black hood stood beside the poor hanging fisherman. The rest of the gnomes were lined up in front, watching. Although she couldn't prove it, Mrs O'Neill knew Alex had been messing with her gnomes and she was the huffiest person on the street as a result.

Today though, when he opened the door, Alex found that Mrs O'Neill wasn't at all angry.

'It's your granny. I'm so sorry, you poor thing.' Her voice was soft; her eyes had tears. 'She's dead. You better come in to my house. There's some people want to talk to you.'

And so began a long boring evening with lots of adults coming to see him: policemen, men in suits, women in suits.

Only when one of the grownups in the house

said that Alex was rich, that he would get all of his granny's money, did he become alert. It was the book again! But this was not what he'd imagined. When he had made the wish he'd thought that he would find a chest full of gold or a suitcase full of cash.

Poor Granny Brady. But it wasn't his fault, Alex told himself, it was the book. That must have been why it'd laughed at him in such an evil way.

Everyone wanted to know how to contact Alex's mum and dad, but Alex pretended he didn't know. He needed time to fix this before worrying his parents.

'Alex, you can stay here tonight,' Mrs O'Neill clasped her hands together and sighed, 'but tomorrow you will go to your new home, a special place for orphans. At least until your parents come back.'

Alex didn't like the sound of that. Those kinds of places didn't let you stay up late playing computer games. As he lay in bed, Alex got fiercely angry with the magic book. It was all very well making him rich, but it was mean to Granny Brady and, what was worse, it was useless if he was going to be stuck in an orphans' home for months.

* * *

At morning break the next day Alex went to the school library. There was a boy already reading near the corner.

'Hey, Bozo. Get out of here!'

'Make me! I was here first.' The boy was brave, but foolish.

Alex took his time, selecting two hardback books of the right weight. All the while the boy watched and a look of alarm appeared on his face. One volume balanced in each hand, Alex closed in on his victim, ready to slam the books against his ears.

'I've finished here anyway.' Dropping his own book to the floor, the boy scrambled off, leaving Alex alone.

Just to be sure, Alex pushed a wedge in the library door, to stop it from opening. Then, ignoring a slight sense of danger, he crawled under the shelf and pulled the magic book from its hiding place. A tingle of fear ran up his arms, making the little hairs there all stand up.

Nevertheless, Alex lifted the heavy volume on to

a desk and turned over the front cover. Strangely, his own writing and the pictures from before had disappeared. There were just blank pages in front of him. Scowling and determined, Alex got out his green pen: **I want my granny back.**

This time the laughter was loud and clear. It was coming from the book.

Annoyed, Alex closed the heavy covers with a bang. So this book liked messing him around, did it? Well nobody messed with Alex Zwick. He had to look after himself in this world and he wasn't going to let a book get the better of him. Let the book laugh as much as it wanted. Alex was determined to get his wishes. And when Alex was determined about something, he got it.

There was no sign of his granny when Alex let himself in to his house that night. Maybe the book couldn't bring people back to life? Maybe there were limits to what you could wish for?

After making himself some beans on toast, Alex had nearly forgotten about his wish. It was after dark and he was sitting in front of the TV when a loud banging on the door made him jump.

Knock … Knock …

'Granny?'

He opened the door and it was her. But she was strange. She walked right in, her eyes didn't seem to be looking anywhere, her arms were straight in front of her, and her legs moved with jerks.

'Food.' Her voice was deep and husky.

'Gran. Don't look at me like that. It's creepy.'

'Food.'

'I know. We have bacon in the fridge.'

'Bacon. Goooood,' she growled happily and, with an odd rocking motion, she went into the kitchen.

'Gran?'

'Hungry.' Her voice was a wheezy whisper. Inside the fridge was a plate of uncooked sausages and bacon. 'Ummmm!' Granny Brady knelt down and began eating them, raw.

'Good.' She nodded at Alex. 'Very good.'

Yuck! thought Alex as he looked at her.

When she had finished the lot, Alex's granny plonked herself in her favourite chair and pointed the remote control at the TV. She flicked through all the channels until she came to an old film with a monster chasing screaming people.

'Mmmm.' She nodded shakily and gave a toothy grin.

'Granny?' Alex stood in front of her, amazed and a little bit alarmed.

Granny Brady didn't answer, but leaned to the side to get a better view of the TV. With a shrug, Alex left her to it. He was annoyed at the book again. This wasn't what he'd meant and the book must've known that. It was probably there below the bookshelves, sniggering away at the fact that Alex now had a zombie granny.

What should I do? Alex wondered. I should tell someone. With a sigh, Alex picked up the phone and dialled a very long number. After it had rung for a while, his dad answered.

'Alex? Is that you? Don't you know it's four in the morning here?'

'Dad, Granny's turned into a zombie.'

'Is that what you got me up to tell me? Look son, I agree with you. I said that myself years ago.'

'No Dad, I mean, she *really* is a zombie. Her voice is all deep and she just ate a plate of raw sausages and bacon.'

'Here, your mum is awake, tell her.'

In the background Alex could just make out his dad grumbling about needing sleep.

'Alex? What's the matter?'

'It's Granny. She's turned into a zombie.' He explained again about the raw meat, but had no intention of mentioning the magic book. That was his secret and, in any case, his mum wouldn't believe him.

'Raw meat? Listen Alex; the doctor's number is in the drawer. Ring it tomorrow and ask him to come over. Right?'

'Right,' replied Alex glumly. The doctor wouldn't do much good. How do you cure someone from being a zombie? If the doctor wasn't careful, Granny Brady would probably try to eat his brains.

'Be good, won't you?'

'No,' said Alex automatically as he hung up.

He left his gran watching horror movies and lay in bed. It was clear that the book was trying to get him into a total mess. Still, if the book thought that was going to make him give up on wishes, it was wrong. He could live with a zombie for a granny, if he had to. It might get a bit smelly. But so long as there was plenty of meat in the fridge, everything would be fine.

With a chuckle to himself, Alex suddenly thought of the good side about having a zombie for a granny. What if he invited some of his classmates over to visit and then set his granny on them to give them a scare? They would all run screaming up the street while Granny Brady lumbered after them. Or perhaps he should invite Mrs O'Neill in for tea. Then, just as she began complaining about Alex again, as she always did, he could release his granny at her! Alex smiled in triumph. Let the book do the worst that it could. He was not going to let the fact that he was living with a zombie put him off making another wish.

Before he turned over and went to sleep, Alex mulled over what he desired next. Ideally, he'd like a pair of football boots that allowed him to score whenever he wanted, but it was risky asking for something like that. The book was bound to try something sneaky. What if the boots became stuck to his feet? Or perhaps caused him to score own-goals, or something? He would have to write the wish out very carefully and cover all the possibilities.

Sleep came as he was working out how to wish for magic football boots. But in his dreams, Alex heard whispers and the sounds of digging. From the roof above him came the patter of rain. But it wasn't raining outside. Some nights you sleep well and don't even notice your dreams. That night, though, without ever quite waking up, Alex threw himself from side to side with terrible nightmares.

5

The Curse Of The Pictures

It was Saturday and Alex lay in bed, trying to get rid of the feeling that something was wrong. Well, perhaps all he was worried about was sharing the house with a zombie. That was the kind of thing that would worry most people. Or was it that he felt the magic book was laughing at him? That also should have been enough to bother anyone.

No, there was something else that made him shiver, something from his dreams.

As he was standing in the bathroom in his space-rocket pyjamas, brushing his teeth, Alex looked at himself in the mirror. It was just as well he did, for in the reflection he saw a dark shadow creep above the bathroom door. Alex stopped brushing.

Something large, deadly and yet very silent was

right behind him near the roof. Not sure about what he'd just seen, Alex braced himself, then, crouching down, he charged out of the door, whirled around and looked back. It turned out that he'd just been quick enough.

A *huge* black spider dropped from the roof and glared at him with horrible clusters of angry eyes. Two enormous teeth, dripping with venom, caught Alex's horrified attention. It was just like the spider he'd drawn in the book, but bigger, more terrible and *very* frightening; especially in the way it raised its front two legs and waved them at Alex.

'Argggggghhhh!' With a scream of terror, Alex scrambled down the stairs, the spider scuttling after him.

They both charged in to the front room, where Granny Brady was still sitting in her chair.

'Food?' asked Alex's granny, looking up eagerly.

Alex pointed a shaky hand behind him, to where the spider was just coming in through the door. His granny got up with a jerk.

The spider didn't like the look of the zombie. It

reared up and backed away from Granny Brady.

With a whoop of relief, Alex immediately recovered from his fright.

'Yes! That's it Granny, breakfast!'

'Breakfast.' Granny lumbered towards the spider, reaching out her pale white arms.

Now you probably don't know what a nervous giant spider looks like, but it kind of sways and its eyes go all shiny with alarm. This one retreated as Granny Brady came towards it. Back up the stairs it went, never turning around, always keeping watch

on the strange creature shuffling towards it over the carpet.

'Go Granny! Go Granny!' Alex was dancing and jumping at a safe distance behind his granny, delighted with the turn of events.

The spider withdrew into the dark safety of the spare room, the one his parents used when they were home. Nipping around his granny, Alex slammed the door shut on the monster and turned the key triumphantly.

'Breakfast?' groaned his granny with disappointment.

'Just give me a moment to dress and we'll go to the butcher's. You deserve a treat for that!'

Not long afterwards, Alex opened the door to a bright Saturday morning. It should have been a very satisfying moment, admiring the new day having triumphed over a fearsome spider, but, once again, he had the feeling that something was wrong. What could it be? Leaning carefully out, he looked above the door, but there was nothing unusual about that. The front garden was very quiet and still, like it was holding its breath. Not even a leaf trembled. Wait, that leaf over there did and that one too. Was there a cat in the bushes?

As Alex took a step out of the front door on to

the path, it gave way. He was falling into a pit and there, underneath him, was a row of sharp wooden spikes.

Luckily, Alex was able to avoid the murderous fall by grabbing on to the sides of the pit. But even so, he was hanging on by his finger tips, dangling above the drop. And then he heard high-pitched voices.

'Hurray! We've got him, boys.'

'Charge!'

Little red hats bobbed in to view. A moment later he could feel a stinging in his fingers. Mrs O'Neill's horrible gnomes were stabbing him with their fishing rods! It took a great effort to put up with the pain, but he had to or he would fall.

'Granny Brady! Help! Help!' Alex yelled.

'Breakfast?' Granny's voice came from some-where behind him.

'Yes, breakfast. Eat them all up!'

'Let's get out of here!' came a shrill yelp. 'Run for it, boys!'

Soon, a firm but cold and clammy hand pulled him up to safety.

With a last shudder of fright, Alex looked down at the dark pit and the terrible spikes.

'I see. Just like my drawing in the book again.' He scowled. 'You'd better watch out!' Alex shouted at the bushes, 'My gran loves eating garden gnomes.'

Beside him, while the bushes shivered and issued frightened squeaking noises, his granny nodded her head.

Up at the butcher's, Alex left his granny outside, drooling at the window display.

'How's Mrs Brady?' asked the butcher politely as he served Alex.

'She's fine. A few more please.' Alex pointed at some beef steaks.

'Right you are, guests for dinner, is it?'

'And ten chops, twenty slices of bacon, all that lamb, all those chicken breasts, oh, we'd better have that mince and that side of ham as well.'

The butcher's jaw dropped open with amazement. Shaking his head, but without saying another word, he filled two bags with Alex's shopping.

Alex and Granny Brady strolled home together, Alex thinking hard, his granny chewing happily on a lamb chop.

'Hi, Alex. Hi, Mrs Brady.'

It was Emily Madden, sitting on the stone wall at the bottom of her auntie's house.

'Hi, Emily.'

Alex didn't have many friends, but he quite liked Emily. She was like him, having to look after herself because her mum and dad weren't around much.

'Why is your granny giving me funny looks?'

Emily dropped off the wall and edged away.

'She got turned into a zombie.'

'Really, wow, yes. She really does look like a zombie now you come to say it. How did that happen?'

For a moment Alex paused. Then he shrugged. 'I found a magic book. It gives you wishes.'

'You wished your granny was a zombie? That's mean, even for you Alex Zwick.'

'No, no. I just wished to be rich. Then I came home and granny was dead. All her money was mine, but I wanted her back. So I wished she was back and she turned up like this.'

'Jeez Louise.'

Emily looked thoughtful and walked alongside Alex.

They came to his granny's house.

'Don't walk on the path; the gnomes next door have dug a spike-filled pit.'

'What?'

'It's the book, see, I drew a picture of a pit. It makes things come alive, I think.'

'Holy Moly! What else did you draw?'

'Oh yeah,' muttered Alex as he entered the house. 'Don't open the spare room. There's a giant venomous spider locked inside.'

'Jeepers Creepers! Can I have a look?'

Alex shook his head. 'I wouldn't risk it.'

Later, Alex and Emily were playing with Alex's new games console.

'So, what are you going to wish for next?' wondered Emily.

'Here.' Alex reached over to the chair beside him and picked up a piece of paper that he'd written on.

'My wish list by Alex Zwick,' Emily read aloud. 'Number one: a pair of magic football boots that always score. Number two: a level one hundred warrior in Endless Battle.' She looked up. 'Isn't, like, the highest level in that game fifty?'

'Exactly,' nodded Alex.

'Three,' Emily continued, 'a special vampire trading card, attack ten thousand, defence ten thousand, immune to all magic, traps and counters.' She rolled her eyes as if to say she thought the wishes were stupid.

'Four: a teleporter so that I only have to step in to it and I come out wherever I want. Now that's a good wish. That's the best one. Could you wish that it works for everyone, so I can use it too.'

'Sure.'

'Cool, we could, like, go to the seaside or some warm place, with ice-creams. Wait, though, how do we get back?'

'That's wish five.'

'I see.' Emily looked back down at the list. 'Five: a portal teleporter, like a wristwatch or something, that zaps me back home. Coola-Boola.

'Six: to be able to fly. Not bad. Seven: that my mum and dad were home more often.'

'Oh.' Alex blushed, 'I forgot I'd written that.'

'It's a good wish. If I had wishes, I would wish I wasn't on my own so often.'

'Yeah.'

For a while, they played the game in silence, thinking about how they were left to themselves, sometimes for months at a time. The noise of the television and the slavering munching of Granny Brady in the background were the only sounds in the house.

'The thing is, Emily, the book is alive.'

'Really?'

'Yeah, it laughs at me. Then it deliberately makes my wishes come out twisted. Like, to get this console, a truck crashed into a shop and blew up. Then there's the spider and the pit. Plus my granny. That book – it's very creepy. It's a bit dangerous and it's really starting to annoy me.'

'Oh, well why don't you leave it alone then?'

'No.' Alex had on his stubborn face. 'I want my wishes, but I want them to be done properly.'

'I'd like to see this book.'

Alex looked at Emily and it felt good to share his secret.

'All right then.'

6

Long-Lost Wishes

Alex and Emily were looking through a fence at the school sports field, to where some older kids were chasing a ball across the mud.

'Great. The changing room will be open. Come on,' urged Alex as he hurried in to the school grounds.

'Are we allowed?'

Emily ran to keep up.

'No.'

'Jeez Louise, Alex, you're terrible.'

No one noticed as they nipped through the changing rooms and in to the school.

It was strange being in school when no one else was around. Silence hung in the corridors and classrooms like the whispers of ghosts. A great rush of noises normally covered the shiny polished floors. Strange too, thought Alex, to be in school without his uniform on. He quite liked the feeling it gave him, like he was free to do whatever he wanted, like there were no more rules.

'This way.'

'Your school is huge.' Emily kept her voice hushed, although there was no one around to hear them.

'I guess.'

'Don't you worry you might get in trouble?' she asked him.

'Not really. I'm always in trouble.'

'Well, what about the book, doesn't that scare you a bit?'

At first Alex was going to boast, because no boy likes to admit to being scared. But he looked back at Emily and saw she was looking from side to side like a frightened rabbit.

'You wish you hadn't come now, don't you?'

Emily nodded.

'It's not far. And yes, I am a bit scared. But look, this is magic, even if it is bad magic. And … Well, I'm glad you're here, I want to show it to you.'

It was true, thought Alex. This would be harder on his own, more frightening. For the first time ever, he admitted to himself that he was glad to have a friend with him.

'All right. Carry on,' Emily responded bravely and Alex smiled at her.

Slowly, quietly, they walked up some worn stairs to a corridor filled with the grey light of a wintry Saturday afternoon. Alex paused and with a nervous smile placed his hand on the brass door-knob of the library.

Inside, the room was as unnaturally still as the rest of the school. Spotting the switch beside the door, Emily reached up.

'Better not. Someone might see the light from outside and come and look.'

It would've been a comfort to have had on the bright strip lights though, for the two children had to move between the shelves with gloomy shadows gathering in the corners of the room.

'There,' Alex whispered fiercely, pointing.

'It's *huge*.'

Together they pulled the book from underneath the shelf and dropped it heavily on to a desk. Emily traced the gold design of the masks with her finger.

'Oh, it tingles.'

Once more Alex opened the book and once more was faced with the huge letters:

What Is It That You Wish For?

'Where are your drawings and wishes?' Emily asked.

'They disappear.'

She leaned over close, and then turned the page, and the next.

'You can nearly see writing, up close.'

Just the faint hint of words and lines survived on the pages. As they leafed through the book though, both Alex and Emily suddenly felt the presence of hundreds of thousands, millions even, of long-lost wishes. Wishes for gold and jewels; wishes for fame; wishes for success in love and war; wishes to visit the moon and wishes to go back in time; wishes for beauty and wishes for strength. All the wishes you can imagine people would make and then more.

'Wow. It really is a magic book,' whispered Emily in awe.

'Yeah.'

They kept turning the pages, touching them, sensing the wishes of those who a long time ago must have written down their desires.

'Are you going to make another wish?' They were about half way through the book when Emily looked up.

'I am. But it's going to try to cheat me. I've got an idea though.' Alex paused, then turned to face the open pages in front of him. 'Listen to me book.' He glanced to check Emily wasn't laughing at him for talking to the book, but she looked very serious. 'I'm going to make a wish. But if anything goes wrong with it, I'm going to tear a few pages out. See?'

With those fierce words Alex took hold of a corner of a page and pulled, intending to rip it. But he couldn't. It was like trying to tear plastic. Worse, the page wasn't even stretching at all.

A chuckle filled the library and the room suddenly seemed very dark.

'Did you hear that?' Emily asked, shocked.

'Yeah, it's really horrible the way it laughs at me.'

Not to be thwarted, Alex brought a box of matches out from his pocket.

'Now pay attention book. I've got matches and I'm not afraid to use them.'

With a hand that was only shaking a small amount, Alex dragged a match along the side of the box until it flared up. He held it against the corner of a page for a long time, until there was no stick left to hold and he had to drop the curled black remains on the desk. But his efforts were as pointless as if he had tried to set fire to glass. Worse again, the page wasn't even warm.

Once more an evil laugh of triumph rang out around them.

'Maybe we should leave it alone?'

Alex shook his head. 'There has to be a way of making this book behave.'

Emily, Alex and *The Book of Curses* sat, or lay, in silence, while the shadows of the room deepened, until the covers of the books all around them became impossible to read in the gloom.

'I know,' said Alex at last. 'Let's find out what happened to everyone else who wrote wishes in the book.'

'How?'

Leaning over the page, Alex began to write.

'Wait, Alex, you probably shouldn't.'

But these were the kinds of words that Alex always ignored. In fact, nothing was more likely to get Alex Zwick to do something than to tell him he shouldn't.

'There.'

I wish I knew what happened to the other people who wrote wishes in this book.

A moment later, Emily pointed at the book with a gasp.

'Look, pictures and they're moving.' But when she turned back to Alex he was gone.

7

Inside The Book
Of Curses

Walking down a cold dry path, Alex felt choked by the dust that was drifting all around him. Where was he? The ground was flat and yellow as far as he could see, but the path was heading towards a distant white stone building.

After walking for a short time, Alex met a man who was resting against a crooked and leafless tree.

'Hello,' said Alex.

The man looked up, tired black eyes in a pale face.

'Where am I?' Alex asked nervously.

The man gave a bitter smile. 'Ah, new are you? Welcome to the desert of lost souls.'

'The desert of lost souls? What's that?'

'It's a place for the dead and the undying, a place for everyone who ever wrote in *The Book of Curses*.'

Alex stopped and mulled this over for a minute.
'You mean a magic book that grants wishes, but in a
twisted way.'

'It grants curses.' The elderly man clenched his
fist. 'It was a cruel day, when I found that book.'

'What did you wish for?' asked Alex curiously.

'What did I wish for? You want to know? Gold,
of course. Everything that I touched, I wanted to
turn into gold. Soon I was rich; I had golden fruit,
chairs, trees, donkeys. You name it. But it was a trap.

As soon as I put my lips to food or drink, they turned to gold. And so I died of thirst and came here, another ghost living in the endless pages of *The Book of Curses*.'

'I see. You wished for everything you touched to turn to gold?' Alex shook his head. 'That was a bit stupid.'

'Why you rascal, how dare you speak to me like that! I was the most powerful king in the world. I would've had you walled up in a dungeon for being so rude.' The old man's anger quickly faded. 'But you're right. It was a stupid wish.'

Alex continued walking, leaving the man sighing beneath the tree. After a while, he came across a woman, no bigger than a baby, whose skin had wrinkles so deep her body looked like the surface of a walnut.

'Hello,' said Alex.

'Hello, young man,' she replied, her voice a frail whisper.

'Why are you here?' Alex asked.

'Ah.' Tears came to her eyes. 'I am cursed, for I

once wished that I would never die. That was over two thou-sand years ago. How I regret it.'

'Let me guess. You wrote that wish in a book, right?'

'An evil book that turned my fear of death in to the thing I desire above all else.'

'I see,' murmured Alex, looking down at the small twisted woman with some pity.

Seeing that even speaking was difficult for her, Alex said goodbye and continued along the path.

When he was about half way to the white palace, Alex came up to a sad-looking cheetah, which was stretched out on the sand. Although the animal didn't look dangerous, he kept well away from it, watching it all the time. He was surprised when the cheetah glanced at him and spoke,

'Hello, little boy.'

'Oh, you can speak?' Alex was surprised.

'Yes,' the cheetah sighed, 'for I was once a man.'

'What happened?' asked Alex.

'I made a wish in a magic book: that I would be the fastest runner in the world. And this is what happened to me.'

'I see,' said Alex.

The cheetah said no more, but laid its head back down on its outstretched paws with another sad sigh, and so Alex continued along the track.

Eventually, Alex reached the great pale building at the end of the path. He walked through tall silent columns of white stone and in to the shadows of an enormous hall. In the middle of the vast chamber was a throne and sitting upon it was a giant man whose head had two faces: one smiling with wickedness, the other frowning with anger. It was impossible to say which face scared Alex the most, but he bravely continued walking until he stood near the sandal of the giant.

'Alex Zwick,' the giant's voice boomed out through the hall like the foghorn of a lighthouse. 'Welcome to my realm.' He turned the smiling face towards Alex and looked down at him.

'Who are you?' Alex asked bravely.

'I am Janus, god of magic.'

'Are you the book?'

'I made the book and I like to visit it from time to time, to enjoy my handiwork.' The god chuckled, with a laugh exactly the same as the one in the library.

'Well, I don't see what's funny here.' Alex narrowed his eyes angrily. 'You've been very mean to everyone.'

'And what's wrong with that?' The god's voice echoed around Alex, long after he had finished speaking.

This was a tough question. It was the kind of question that Alex used to ask when people told him he'd been bad. What was wrong with being mean to everyone?

'You've made a lot of people very, very sad,' Alex answered, eventually. 'But why am I here?'

'Your wish, remember? "I wish I knew what happened to the other people who wrote wishes in this book." Well, I've given you what you wanted. And when you have spoken to everyone here, I'll let you go. But you know what?' The god laughed again.

'What?'

'There are too many people here and more arrive each day. So you'll never finish. Ha ha ha!' Janus's triumphant cries bellowed through the room.

To be fair to Alex, even though he was very scared by the huge god, that part of him which said 'no' to his parents, his granny, his teacher, to Mrs O'Neill and many others – the stubborn part of him – refused to lie down.

'I'll find a way to beat you!' shouted Alex.

'Oh I don't think so,' replied the god and turned his angry face towards Alex. For a moment the world went dark and the fury of a storm seemed to break out all around. And then the god was gone.

In a way, Alex was right. Something in him did defeat *The Book of Curses*. But it was Emily who should really get the credit for what happened next.

8

An Impossible Wish

Emily, you will remember, had been left alone in the dark library. The only light by this time was the glow from the book, which had come alive in front of her. Every page told the story of how someone had made a wish, but although it came true, they were cursed as a result. And, magically, there seemed to be thousands of pages.

Tearing herself away from the stories, Emily turned to the very last page, at the back of the book. There, she saw Alex, a tiny figure. Rather bravely and stubbornly, he was standing up to a giant with two faces. But all around her was a mocking chuckle.

What should she do? She desperately wanted to help Alex escape the trap he was in.

There was no point running off to ask someone else. This was magic and no teacher could help with that.

Looking at her friend, so small, but so defiant, Emily had an idea. And the more she thought about it, the more she liked it.

It took both hands to turn the book over and open it again at the front page. There, under the words 'What Is It That You Wish For?' she wrote in pencil:

I wish that Alex Zwick was a good, well-behaved boy.

All at once the laughter ended and the book slammed shut with a choking sound. Then it began to cough and splutter. The pages fluttered. A groaning sound filled the library and the book trembled on the table, like someone trying to lift a weight far too heavy for them. Steam poured out of the book and the groaning got louder and louder and louder.

At last, with a cry of despair, there was a great flash. All the pages of the book flew apart, scattering like golden leaves in a storm. For a moment they filled the library with a bright light, which faded away as they melted to nothing.

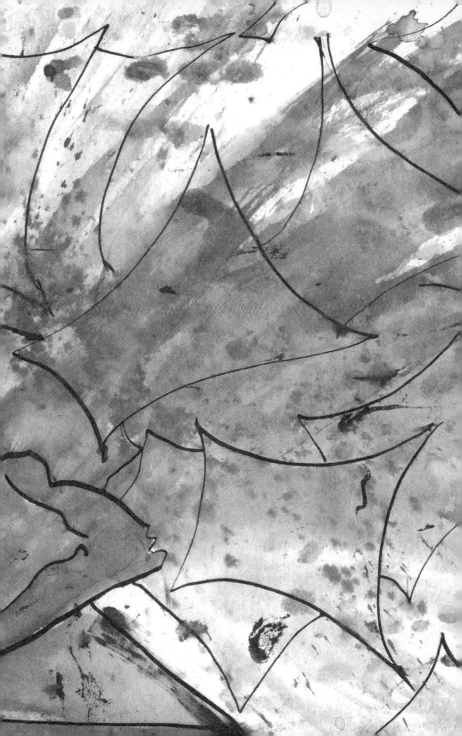

Even the big, thick, leather covers were rotting fast and there, back in the library, his hair standing all on end, was Alex Zwick.

'Jeepers Alex, am I glad to see you!'

'What happened?' Alex blinked a few times.

'I wished that you were a good, well-behaved boy.'

'Ahhh,' Alex nodded, and then smiled. 'I felt something tugging inside me. But I wouldn't budge.' Alex paused thoughtfully. 'You know that was a clever wish – a wish that the book couldn't cope with.'

'Thanks.'

Emily and Alex shared a glance of triumph.

'Mind you,' Alex suddenly frowned, 'I can't get any more wishes now.'

'Tut, tut.' Emily shook her head from side to side. 'You're hopeless, Alex. You should be grateful to have escaped.'

'I know. But that's the way I am.'

'What do you think happened to the other people in the book, like the ancient woman and the cheetah? Did they escape too?'

'I think so. Everything fell apart and we were all flung in to the sky. When I landed, I was here and I guess they went back to where they came from too.'

'I hope so.'

'And me,' replied Alex.

This made Emily smile. 'Maybe my wish worked after all.'

'What?'

'You're turning nice, Alex Zwick.'

'No,' said Alex automatically. 'It's just that I want that god, Janus, to be really upset and the more people who escaped the better.'

'Jeez Louise, Alex, you're terrible.'

'Come on, we'd better leave. It's getting dark.' Alex sounded gruff, but he gave Emily a warm smile.

* * *

Back at Alex's house, all the gnomes had returned to their places in Mrs O'Neill's garden.

'That's interesting,' said Alex and Emily nodded in agreement.

Instead of going in to his house, Alex went through the side door and got a rake from around the back. Then he carefully prodded at the path in front of him. Nothing strange happened. It was completely normal. There was no pit.

'Alex! There you are!' The front door opened and out came Alex's mum and dad.

'Hello, Emily. Now what's this about Granny being sick?' Alex's mum continued without waiting for them to reply, 'she's perfectly well.'

'Really?' Alex looked up curiously and there was Granny Brady, full of health, waving at him from the door. He glanced at Emily who nodded. Destroying the book had broken the curse.

'Coola-Boola,' Emily whispered, 'she's back to how she was.'

'Yeah, but does that mean I've lost my games console?' Alex grumbled. 'Mum, Gran, can Emily come in and play for a bit?'

'Of course she can dear.' Granny Brady was back

to her good-natured self.

'Until tea,' added Alex's mum, primly.

Inside the house, Alex's dad was sitting on the sofa, watching the football results. There was no sign of the games console.

'Hi, Dad.'

'Hi, Alex.'

'What are you doing home?' Alex asked.

'Your mum got worried about your phone call. Anyway, we thought we hadn't seen you for a while and we'd work from home for the next year or two.'

'Oh.' Alex stood for a while in thought.

'Have you been in your old room?'

'Yes. Why?' His dad suddenly sounded suspicious, 'were you playing in it?'

'No. It's just that I locked a giant venomous spider in there.'

'Well, it's not there now.'

'That's a relief.' Alex said, although with a slight tone of disappointment.

'Would you like some sandwiches, dear?' Granny Brady and Alex's mum came back in to the room. Alex's dad turned up the volume on the TV.

'No thanks. Come on Emily, let's play out the back.'

'Just a moment, Alex,' said his mum, 'aren't you glad to see us?'

'Actually,' Alex paused, before continuing to his own surprise, 'I am.'

'That's nice.' His mum leant over and gave him a hug, while his dad gave a nod of approval.

'Now go and play. And be good, won't you?'

'No,' said Alex Zwick and shot away.

*　　*　　*

But the truth is Alex Zwick was never quite as stubborn and annoying as he used to be. He was especially nice to Emily, who he played with nearly every weekend. Perhaps some of her wish had rubbed off on him. Or perhaps he had learned something from the time he had been inside *The Book of Curses*.

WATCH OUT FOR THE FORBIDDEN FILES!

THE WITCH APPRENTICE

Marian Broderick

What if you were adopted by WITCHES?

There's something **very** odd going on in Anna Kelly's new home – her guardians, Grizz and Wormella Mint, are **witches**, and they want Anna to help them with their nasty spells! So Anna's stuck in their horrible house, chopping up **toadstools** and scrambling **frogspawn**, with no one but Charlie the cat for company. Is there **any** way out for her? But then she finds an **evil, old spell book** in the cellar – can Anna make the magic work for **her?**

ISBN: 978-1-84717-039-2

THE EVIL HAIRDO

Oisín McGann

'None of this was my fault!'

It all started with my favourite girl band: *WitchCraft*. They were beautiful. They could sing and dance and above all … they were *cool*. And I wanted the *Witchcraft* hairdo – more than **anything** else in the world. But then I got it, and that's when the trouble started. Because it turned out that my hair was **evil** …

My name is Melanie, I'm ten years old, and this is my story.

ISBN: 978-0-86278-940-4

THE POISON FACTORY
Oisín McGann

Meet the living dead, giant insects and the man with the most disgusting job in the world!

When Gaz loses his football *and* his little brother Joey, there's nothing for it but to go into the **spooky** chemical factory and Gaz, Hayley and Damo soon find themselves up to their necks in trouble. Will they find Joey, or will they meet a **terrifying** fate?

ISBN: 978-0-86278-941-1